Published on the occasion
of the exhibition *About Face*
Hayward Gallery, London
24 June – 5 September 2004

Exhibition curated by William A. Ewing,
Nathalie Herschdorfer and Jean-Christophe Blaser,
Musée de l'Elysée, Lausanne
Organised by Musée de l'Elysée, Lausanne, with the
generous support of Culturgest, Lisbon, and Pro Helvetia

Hayward Gallery showing organised by Emma Mahony

Catalogue designed by UNA (London) designers
Art Publisher: Caroline Wetherilt
Publishing Co-ordinator: James Dalrymple
Sales Manager: Deborah Power
Printed in Italy by Mondadori

Cover: Inez van Lansweerde/Vinoodh Matadin, *Kirsten*,
1997 (cat.63) (detail)
Page 1 and 88: LawickMüller, *Apollo from Olympia – Oliver* and
Athena Velletri – Nina from the series *PERFECTLY superNATURAL*,
1999 (cat.69, 71) (details)

Published by Hayward Gallery Publishing, London SE1 8XX, UK
© Hayward Gallery 2004
Texts © the authors 2004
Artworks/photographs © the artists 2004 (unless otherwise stated)

ISBN 1 85332 243 1

Hayward Gallery Publishing titles are distributed outside
North and South America by Cornerhouse Publications,
70 Oxford Street, Manchester M1 5NH
Telephone +44 (0)161 200 1503
Facsimile +44 (0)161 200 1504
Email publications@cornerhouse.org
www.cornerhouse.org/publications

About Face
Photography and the Death of the Portrait

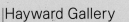
Hayward Gallery

1 about face:
phrase, Concerning the
subject of the face
2 about face:
v., A military command:
to face oppositely; to
turn 180 degrees
3 about-face:
n., The act of facing
oppositely; a reversal of
attitude or point of view

Preface

We live in an age where plastic and reconstructive surgery are commonplace, where miracle drugs and genetic engineering beckon, and where a multi-million dollar advertising industry promotes an often singular, ideal view of beauty. As the human face is restructured by science, advances in new media and computer technologies enable it to be re-thought and re-imagined by artists and photographers. *About Face* brings together works that reflect upon scientific and genetic advances, posits a new approach to the photographic portrait and questions our faith in photographic truth.

About Face extends the Hayward Gallery's active involvement in exhibitions that push boundaries and explore timely and provocative new territories. It raises many fascinating questions and makes some bold assertions about the future of the photographic portrait, based on the perspective of 70 international artists, photographers and photo journalists, some of whom don't even use a camera, preferring instead to work with found imagery which they alter accordingly.

About Face has been originated by the Musée de l'Elysée in Lausanne and was first shown at Culturgest, Lisbon, as *Cara a Cara* (Face to Face), before returning to the Musée de l'Elysée where it was shown in two parts as *Je t'envisage* (I see/imagine you). Our thanks go first and foremost to William A. Ewing, Director of the Musée de l'Elysée, for conceiving and curating this exhibition with characteristic curiosity and insightfulness and for his thorough and illuminating essay in this publication. We also extend our thanks to his colleagues at Musée de l'Elysée, particularly Associate Curators Jean-Christophe Blaser and Nathalie Herschdorfer, who assisted him with all aspects of the exhibition. *About Face* owes a debt of gratitude to the artists who have agreed to participate in it, and to the lenders of works, institutions and individuals listed on p.87, who have been so generous and supportive of the project; we deeply appreciate their interest and commitment.

This publication has been designed by Nick Bell and Sam Blok of UNA, and we thank them for their energy, dedication and innovative approach to its design. I am, as ever, grateful to Caroline Wetherilt, the Hayward's Art Publisher, and James Dalrymple, our Publishing Co-ordinator, who have brought their expertise and scrupulous attention to the editing and production needs of this 'magazine'.

A great many Hayward staff have been involved in the practical organisation of *About Face,* and I would like to extend my thanks and gratitude to them all. In particular, I would like to thank Martin Caiger-Smith, Head of Exhibitions, who opened discussions with the Musée de l'Elysée about the possibility of a London showing, and who has guided the development of the exhibition throughout, and Emma Mahony, the Hayward Exhibition Organiser responsible for bringing the exhibition to fruition here. Both Martin and Emma worked closely with William Ewing on the selection of the works for the Hayward. Clare van Loenen, our Head of Public Programmes, and her team have devised an engaging and informative programme of talks and events to complement the show. I am very grateful to them, to Avril Scott, the Hayward's Head of Marketing, and her team, and to Ann Berni, Press Relations Manager, and Eleanor Bryson, Press Relations Co-ordinator, in our Press Office. In terms of logistical arrangements, my thanks go to our Registrar, Imogen Winter, Keith Hardy, our Head of Operations, as well as to the technical team. We are delighted to have been able to bring this exciting and timely exhibition to the attention of national and international audiences in London.

Susan Ferleger Brades
Director, Hayward Gallery

The Faces in the Mirror

William A. Ewing
with Jean-Christophe Blaser and Nathalie Herschdorfer

The human body has been at the forefront of art for two decades, and has made for a particularly vigorous vein of art photography. During this period the venerable genre of the nude – for more than a century the only acceptable treatment of the human body in art photography – gradually faded into irrelevance as photographers came to grips with the fact that the body was a messy affair of flesh, secretions, excretions and blood, rather than a set of sinuous female contours to be rearranged *ad infinitum* – and that older women (and men!) had bodies too. Like everyone else, photographers observed that the human body was on the cusp of truly radical change, most notably due to spectacular advances in medicine, genetic engineering and the not-so-distant prospects of human cloning and artificial intelligence. Because the body was being remade by scientists and engineers, it was only natural that artists and photographers would re-imagine it.

The widespread anxiety at the core of all body-centered photography was also, of course, triggered by more immediate concerns: the onslaught of AIDS and the appearance of virulent new microbes, debates over abortion, the increasingly routine transplantation of organs, the manufacture of artificial body parts, and so on. The feeling of disembodiment that all these developments engendered was also reinforced by the psychologically distancing effect of new media and computer technologies. Such anxieties have been fueled by the relentless barrage of advertising – more sophisticated with every passing day – which aims to convince us of our bodily inadequacies. *Your body is a battleground*, a 1989 poster by Barbara Kruger, succinctly summarised the bodily angst of this era (fig.1).

This wave of body-centered photography appears to be receding, and attention is now shifting to the face. And because the face is today as strongly contested politically, economically and culturally as the body was ten or twenty years ago, the face is displacing the narrow genre of the portrait just as the body displaced that of the nude.

Face is, of course, *body*. But the issues that body photographers dealt with were rooted in the flesh – indeed, faces were often purposely not shown (as, for example, in the work of John Coplans (fig.2)). The face photographers, on the other hand, are more concerned with social issues: identity, rootedness, communication and a range of cultural phenomena, most notably an obsessive interest in 'beauty', which appears to be evolving universally towards a homogeneous appearance, and the spectacular, seemingly worldwide, rise of a celebrity culture. Moreover, they are acutely aware of the specificity of their medium, photography.

Because the term 'face' encompasses a domain far broader than is suggested by the word 'portrait', and because the latter term carries so much historical baggage, a growing number of contemporary photographers reject conventional portraiture. Some consider it to have exhausted its powers, endlessly recycling stereotypes and clichés; others see it as a genre fraught with discredited assumptions – both concerning the nature of the face itself, *and* the manner of its representation.

Figure 1
Barbara Kruger.
Untitled (Your body is a battleground), 1989
photographic silkscreen on vinyl; 284 x 284 cm
The Broad Art Foundation

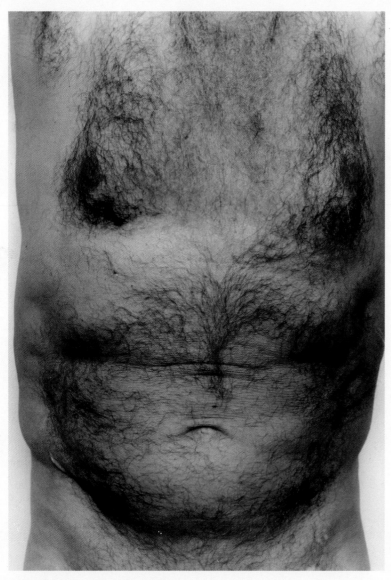

Figure 2
John Coplans.
Self-portrait: Torso Front, 1984
gelatin silver print; 81 x 68 cm
Institut d'art contemporain,
Collection Frac Rhône-Alpes, Villeurbanne
© Estate of John Coplans
and Andrea Rosen Gallery, New York

The photographers featured in *About Face* have two fundamental criticisms of the conventional portrait. The first concerns the claim that the traditional portrait captures or reveals 'the inner being', the personality, the character or 'the soul' of the subject. Their second complaint is that a portrait is falsely assumed to be credible, and a sufficiently complete likeness, of a given individual.

The belief that the portrait can claim to reveal the soul is either dismissed outright by these photographers or categorised as myth. They find fault with this age-old concept for many different reasons: the absolute discreditation of theories of physiognomy (which hold that a person's character and personality can be divined by reading the features of the face); the fawning and the flattery implicit in the client/supplier relationship which characterises any portrait sitting; the fraction-of-a-second that registers a person on film; the uniform high-focus or hyper-realism of portraits (which is not at all consistent with how the eyes see and how the brain reads and interprets faces); and a range of assumptions about 'appropriate' poses and expressions for portraiture. These are some of the key factors that have pushed the current generation of image-makers to either seek new techniques to deal with the face or resuscitate old ones which have fallen out of favour as a result of the dominance of the mainstream portrait. Indeed, what was necessary, some of the photographers argued, was a complete reappraisal – to a large extent, an 'about-face'.

As for the concept of a 'likeness', these photographers are all too aware of the range of manipulative procedures that stand between the sitter and the final image. While it is true that manipulation has always been a factor in portraiture (the first clients were quick to demand retouching and the photographers were happy to oblige), the computer has made seamless transformation easy, fast and cheap – in other words, universal and commonplace. Doubt is now everywhere apparent where individual portraits of *any* kind are concerned. To cite two vivid cases from recent events: Iraqis scorned the pictures of Saddam's dead sons as 'American fabrications', while Americans scoffed at pictures of Saddam himself as 'body doubles'. On a lighter note, we read that French music executives have decided to launch a new star – 'Cherie' – by 'imaging' her in a slot 'no one else was trying to fill ... between Britney Spears and Shania Twain.'[1]

Cynicism has become standard fare for both producers and consumers of images. Not surprisingly, therefore, the artist-photographers of the new 'face' imagery construct their work in a spirit of scepticism (though often laced with subversive humour), founded on the observation that illusions and falsehoods abound. They have broken with the old photographic faith of taking images at 'face value'. British artist John Hilliard, for example, prefers to speak of '...*anti-portraits*, in the sense that they largely refuse or subvert the conventions of the genre.'[2] 'Photography is our exorcism,' proposed Jean Baudrillard. 'Primitive society had its masks, bourgeois society had its mirrors, we have our images.'[3] And Marshall McLuhan observed that 'the field of battle' was shifting from the material world to 'mental image-making *and image–breaking*.'[4]

To understand the significance of this break, we have to look back over 160 years of photographic practice, and beyond, to the history of the mirror image, a necessary condition in the development of self-awareness – or, quite literally, self-reflection.

The modern mirror dates from the mid-sixteenth century, when the Venetians of

...the face is displacing the narrow genre of the portrait just as the body displaced that of the nude.

Murano compressed a layer of mercury between a sheet of glass and a sheet of metal, allowing for perfect, distortion-free reflections. Over the next two centuries, the new mirrors replaced the much inferior bronze and pewter variety, though they remained almost exclusively the property of royalty and the nobility. In fact, it appears that the vast majority of people in even the most advanced countries were not truly familiar with their own faces until the mid-nineteenth century, when mirrors began to filter downwards. Evidence for this is found in the contemporary accounts of the Parisian photographer Nadar, who was stunned to find that when his overwhelmed clerk occasionally handed clients the wrong portraits, they rarely noticed the mistake, even after close examination of the prints. Indeed, they often expressed delight at the fidelity of the portrayals! But the initial reaction of *all* his sitters was the same: 'one of shock'.[5] They were stunned by their images, finding it impossible to hide either their intense pleasure or their extreme disappointment. The majority of Nadar's clients were coming, literally, face-to-face with their own likenesses for the first time in their lives. Anthropologist Edmund Carpenter, referring to native peoples seeing mirror images of themselves for the first time, proposes that: 'The notion that man possesses, in addition to his physical self, a symbolic self, is widespread, perhaps universal …A mirror corroborates this. It does more: it reveals the symbolic self *outside* the physical self. The symbolic self is suddenly explicit, public, vulnerable. Man's initial response to this is probably always traumatic.'[6] The relatively recent arrival of the mirror explains, therefore, the prevalence of mirror metaphors used in the mid-nineteenth century to describe the newly-invented photograph – 'mirror with a memory', 'the mirror of nature' and 'permanent mirror'. Given the reverence for technical progress in the age, it was not surprising that photography was seen not only as a mirror, but as the best kind of mirror ever invented. In London, George Cruikshank celebrated the opening of the first public portrait studio, in Regent Street, with this verse:

Your image reversed will minutely appear
So delicate, forcible, brilliant and clear
So small, full, and round, with a life so
profound
As none ever wore
In a mirror before.[7]

The fact that daguerreotypes, the earliest photographs, were actually highly-polished, silver-coated metal plates encouraged mirror metaphors, as did the fact that the early portrait studios often used a series of mirrors to direct light onto the faces to be photographed.

As photography historian Ben Maddow observes, the *photographic* portrait represented, '…a profoundly new phenomenon …not only an art but a new form of human consciousness.'[8] Painted and drawn portraits had, of course, been around for centuries, but they had been restricted to the upper classes. The arrival of paper prints in the 1850s, followed by the arrival soon after of the tiny, cheaper *carte de visite,* offered all but the poorest inhabitants of industrialised societies the opportunity to have their likenesses made.

There was little talk of capturing 'the soul' in these early years. People simply wanted to know *what they looked like.* Within a decade, however, virtually everyone had his or her own portrait and had seen countless others, and it began to dawn on people how stultifyingly alike the faces appeared. What had previously struck people as unique and marvellous began to strike them as common and uninspired. Clients began to demand something more

The belief that the portrait can claim to reveal the soul is either dismissed outright by these photographers or categorised as myth.

Figure 3
Yousuf Karsh.
Ernest Hemingway, 1957
gelatin silver print; 99 x 73.6 cm
Camera Press Ltd, London
© 1957 Yousuf Karsh

profound, something that would relate to the rich language of physiognomy, the extremely popular and deeply rooted tradition of reading faces for signs of character and personality. Professional portrait photographers, shrewdly realising that they could charge more for this quality, began to adopt 'artistic techniques' (and bigger formats which made faces easier to scrutinise), together with an ennobling discourse to promote their new products. Great claims began to be made for the capacity of the photographic portrait to reveal the soul, or inner being, behind the façade. Ambitious photographers named their studios 'The Palace of Portraiture' or 'The Temple of Photography'.

In practical terms, this meant appealing to the client's self-image, to what they *wanted* to look like. Portrait photographers learned that they would have to lie, discretely, if they were to retain their clients – smearing Vaseline on the lens to blur wrinkles, employing a soft-focus lens to disguise a double-chin, lighting the face to obscure blemishes. And when the photographer's bag of studio tricks was exhausted, the retoucher was called in. As photography historian Helmut Gernsheim wryly observed: 'The public's notions of refinement could not be satisfied without the obliteration of what was characteristic and true.'[9]

The idea that a successful portrait is one that captures or reveals the soul has proven astonishingly resilient. Today's public is as avid for portraits of people it already 'knows' as were people of the nineteenth century, reading into the portrait the traits of character and personality it wants to see. Yousuf Karsh's twentieth-century portraits of 'great' men and women were the inevitable product of physiognomic theories, the peak of the genre. His Ernest Hemingway *was* 'The Old Man and the Sea' (fig.3); his Winston Churchill *was* the rock that had held England fast in the storm. Karsh was, of course, unique only in the relentless way he pursued the famous names; photography collections around the world are cluttered with 'sensitive' portrayals of the great and the good. But the resilience of the Art-encrusted portrait does not impress the new photographers of the face, who are far more likely to be inspired by the 'lowly' passport photo, the unpretentious four-for-a pound photo-booth pictures, the refreshingly direct police mug shot, the vacuous glamour of a Warhol silkscreen 'Marilyn', or the dazzling faces of the eternal Lolitas cloned by the fashion magazines.

New strategies of representation are called for in photography because the nature of the face itself has changed. In an era when facial reconstruction and remodelling has become routine; when 'nutricosmetics' promise to deliver beauty in pills; when whole facial transplants are within the realm of possibility; when genetic engineering promises designer faces (undoubtedly with the brand name tattooed in the skin); and when nanotechnology proposes to replace banal reality with artificial images projected directly on the iris; artists are pushed to their limits imagining the future of the face, let alone dealing with its present realities.

The new photographers of the face are also well aware of the fact that most of the photographed faces that surround us on a daily basis are of a different order from our own: two-dimensional, superhuman in scale, smiling down on us from countless billboards, radiating good health and eternal youth from the pages of 'glossy' magazines. These faces are far more beautiful than the pitifully natural ones that we confront everyday – more confident, happier, immune to stress and the horrors of ageing and, above all, reassuringly familiar, thanks to constant media drip. That these faces are idealised at every stage of production and dissemination – from the selection of the 'right' model through the application of make-up; from the photographic act to the retouching of the resulting image; from the film to the printer's plate and from the plate to the final appearance on the magazine page – is a fact that passes unnoticed by the consumer, but not the artist.

How, then, do the new photographers of the face approach their subjects? *About Face* makes clear that there are as many strategies as there are photographers. There is no actual 'school' as such, but there are common threads to the approaches.

About the nature of the face itself, these photographers believe:

+ That the face is malleable, plastic and capable of being transformed via a gamut of new technologies, in ways that can obliterate its original form; i.e. the face is no longer a fixed entity, one's destiny, an object that one is obliged to carry through life fundamentally unchanged.
+ That the face is a fluid field rather than a fixed object. It changes constantly, from second to second, its musculature providing for thousands of individual expressions which are consciously and unconsciously adopted.
+ That facial gestures and expressions are largely cultural and social constructs rather than a universal language.
+ That race and gender are in large part cultural and social constructs rather than fixed biological properties; or rather that the biological factors are relatively superficial.
+ That although physiognomy has been thoroughly discredited, its tenacious hold on the popular imagination limits the furthering of our understanding and appreciation of the human face.
+ That facial beauty is, contrary to conventional wisdom, an indication of proximity to a mean, or average, rather than a question of exception.
+ That for all its particularities, the face is a part of the body, and not of a higher order – sacred where the body is profane.
+ That although we think we see faces, objectively, in an identical way, faces are in fact fields of data that are interpreted and processed by the brain according to individual needs and experiences, and therefore seen and judged differently by people.

About the nature of photography they believe:

+ That a photograph is made, not taken.
+ That a single image, made at a fraction of a second, can only pretend to represent the fluid field of a human face.
+ That a single image can never claim to retain all the complexity of a human being (i.e. capture or reveal 'the soul').
+ That the act of photographing a face is a complex transaction between artist and subject, involving conscious and unconscious negotiations, and that this give-and-take leaves a trace in the resulting image.
+ That retouching is not a means of hiding truths, as with conventional portraiture, but is instead a means of telling them.
+ That overt and covert techniques of manipulation negate standard notions of credibility, but open the door wide to creative work.
+ That we are increasingly manipulated by the media who have engineered faces (whether generated manually or electronically) to become tools of control and persuasion.

...the artist-photographers of the new 'face' imagery construct their work in a spirit of scepticism...

+ That words that accompany an image radically influence the 'reading' of the image, even to the point of a 180-degree shift in meaning.

Beyond the groupings of the images proposed later on in this publication (Facing Up, Facing Down, etc.), the photographers in *About Face* can also be categorised in terms of adopting four basic positions. In the first category are the photographers that begin with a face as he or she finds it – the face is not made-up, painted, or disguised in any way by the photographer (though it may well be by its owner). They then photograph it in a straightforward manner, no distortion is introduced during the photographic act, or afterwards in the treatment of film and print. Philippe Bazin's studies of the faces of newborn babies are one example (cat.9), as are the studiously neutral faces of the subjects of Thomas Ruff's monumental portraits (cat.107–108).

Secondly, other photographers in *About Face* manipulate the face *itself* in some way – veiling, disguising, masking and painting or drawing upon faces or employing look-a-likes and actors – but photograph it in a straightforward fashion. Alison Jackson's 'portraits' of the Royal Family employ astonishingly convincing doubles (cat.44–45), but she can argue that her actual photographs are simply documents of what is in front of her lens. Hee Jin Kang applies make-up to his male subjects whom he then photographs straightforwardly (cat.47–49).

In the third category are the photographers that begin with a face, which is presented in a straightforward fashion, then manipulate standard photographic processes by means of blur, double- or multiple-exposure, retouching, composites and complex computer interventions. Kathy Grove, for

example, uses professional retouching techniques to transform a twentieth-century icon – Dorothea Lange's *Migrant Mother* – intentionally giving her a slightly repellent plastic look (cat.35). Jiří David purchases stock agency images of the world's leaders, then gives them red eyes and (his own) tears by computer and hand retouching (cat.16).

Lastly, other photographers manipulate or transform the face itself, *and* manipulate the photographic process by retouching, darkroom manipulation or computer intervention. The French artist Orlan is in a class of her own in this regard. Orlan first came to fame for having subjected her face to plastic surgery for artistic ends; in the 'self-hybridisations' shown in *About Face* (cat.91–92), she uses computer manipulation to blend her own, already-transformed features with pre-Columbian sculpture.

There are other artists in *About Face* whose work falls outside of these categories and can not be easily classified. How, for example, should Gary Schneider's larger-than-life faces be classified (cat.112)? They are straight photographs in one sense, but they deviate from the conventional portrait in the manner of their execution – 30- or 40-minute time exposures of faces in total darkness, save for a light-pen that the photographer wields like a brush. As a result, the faces have a strange asymmetry, having registered subtle, involuntary movements. Although this means that we are seeing these people as we would never see them in reality, they are no more 'distortions' of reality than a traditional portrait; they are as faithful to photography as any photograph can be. It is simply that we are not used to seeing faces depicted in this manner.

Emmanuelle Purdon's *Femmes de Mystère* (cat.94–99) – female faces she recuperates

New strategies of representation are called for in photography because the nature of the face itself has changed.

from paintings of the past – are also difficult to categorise. On the canvasses where she first finds them they are already representations, but by photographing the women in grainy black-and-white (thus disguising give-away texture), she restores them to the world of the living and catapults them from past centuries into the present age, where they become vaguely familiar stars of the silver screen. But while the transformations are highly imaginative, Purdon's photography itself is 'straight'.

A number of other artists in *About Face* choose not to touch a camera, preferring instead to work with found imagery. John Stezaker, for example, hunts through family magazines for photographs of invariably happy children and with the subtlest of techniques transforms them from angels to demons (cat.117–119). Martin Parr, a much-travelled photographer, has over the years visited dozens of professional photostudios abroad to have his portrait 'taken' (as opposed to 'made') (cat.93). Parr never touched the cameras that made these portraits, nor did he direct the photographers' work. Yet, taken together, the wildly disparate styles comprise both a homage to a kind of universal folk-art and a paradoxical *self-*portrait unified by the one thing they have in common – their subject's deadpan expression.

Large-scale faces are often assumed to be something new to photography. Few know that André Adolphe Eugene Disderi, inventor of the tiny *carte-de-visite* portrait, also made portraits six-feet tall in the 1860s. 'Mammoth photos' like Disderi's were all the rage in 1860–61, according to Helmut Gernsheim.[10] Although we have become used to seeing gargantuan faces since the arrival of cinema, and though we have come to expect them in outdoor publicity, the same scale is unsettling when faces are displayed indoors,

as with photographic artworks. Thomas Ruff has perplexed critics with his large faces, which are dismissed as overblown passport photographs, conveying nothing as to personality or character (cat.107–108). But that's the point, Ruff suggests: there is nothing beyond what is shown. By printing so big, he challenges us to *look* into the void; perhaps there we will see a way forward. Ruff's photographs do what all photographs do – they map a terrain, and they map it with a precision that no other tool or art can match. Why do we cling to the ludicrous notion of the portrait? Why can't we accept photographs at face value? 'If indeed there is a terrible nihilism in the photograph', warned Marshal McLuhan in 1970, 'then we are surely not the worse for knowing it.'[11] The photographers in *About Face* might argue that in confronting this nihilism, and working through it, they are restoring something of the old magic of the mirror.

William A. Ewing is working on the first full-scale study of the face in contemporary photography, to be published by Thames & Hudson in 2005.

Notes
1   John Seabrook, 'The Money Note', *The New Yorker,* 7 July 2003, pp. 48-49
2   John Hilliard, 'The Picture Within', *Next Level*, no. 4, London, 2003, p. 52
3   Jean Baudrillard, *Car l'illusion ne s'oppose pas à la réalité*, Paris, Descartes, 1998, p. 3
4   Marshall McLuhan, *Understanding Media, the Extensions of Man* (1964), Corte Madera, CA, Gingko Press, 2003, p. 142
5   Nadar, *Quand j'étais photographe* (1900), Actes Sud/Babel, 1998, pp. 45-51
6   Edmund Carpenter, *Oh What a Blow that Phantom Gave Me!,* Chicago/San Francisco, Holt, Rinehart and Winston, 1972-73, p. 143
7   Quoted in *Camera: A Victorian Eyewitness,* London, Gus Macdonald, B.T. Batsford, 1979, p. 22
8   Ben Maddow, *Faces: A Narrative History of the Portrait in Photography*, Boston, New York Graphic Society, 1977, p. XI
9   Helmut Gernsheim, *The History of Photography,* New York/ St Louis/San Francisco, McGraw-Hill, 1969, p. 234
10 Helmut Gernsheim, *The History of Photography,* New York/ St Louis/San Francisco, McGraw-Hill, 1969, p. 315
11 Marshall McLuhan, ibid, p. 262

Facing Up

In *Facing Up* the photographer is in control,
and the subjects are exposed and vulnerable.
Many surrender willingly to the camera's gaze,
facing up to reality; others are in no position
to resist – either they are caught off guard or
they are simply unaware of the camera.
On occasion, the photographers assume both
roles, turning the camera on themselves. There is
no attempt at defence, no pose, no 'keeping up
appearances': emotions, frailties, the marks of
time – from the cradle to the grave – are laid bare
for all to see.

Lee Friedlander. *Finland*, 1995 [31]

Above **Thomas Ruff.** *Portrait (A. Koschkarow)*, 1999 [108]
Right **Judith Joy Ross.** *P.F.C. Maria I. Leon, U.S. Army Reserve, On Red Alert, Gulf War*, 1990 [101]

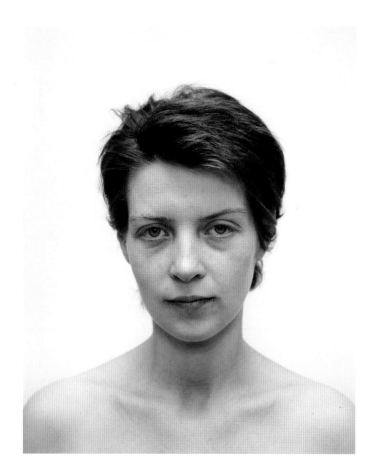 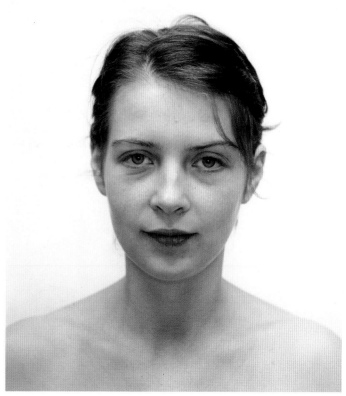

Left **Rineke Dijkstra.** *Tia, Amsterdam, June 23,* 1994 [21]
Right **Rineke Dijkstra.** *Tia, Amsterdam, November 14,* 1994 [22]

Choose ten accomplished photographers. Have them each make a portrait of the same individual. One or two at the most will have produced a portrait which we can instantly recognise. With the other eight, we will not be sure that it is of the same person.
Grand Dictionnaire Slatkine, Geneva, 1866-79

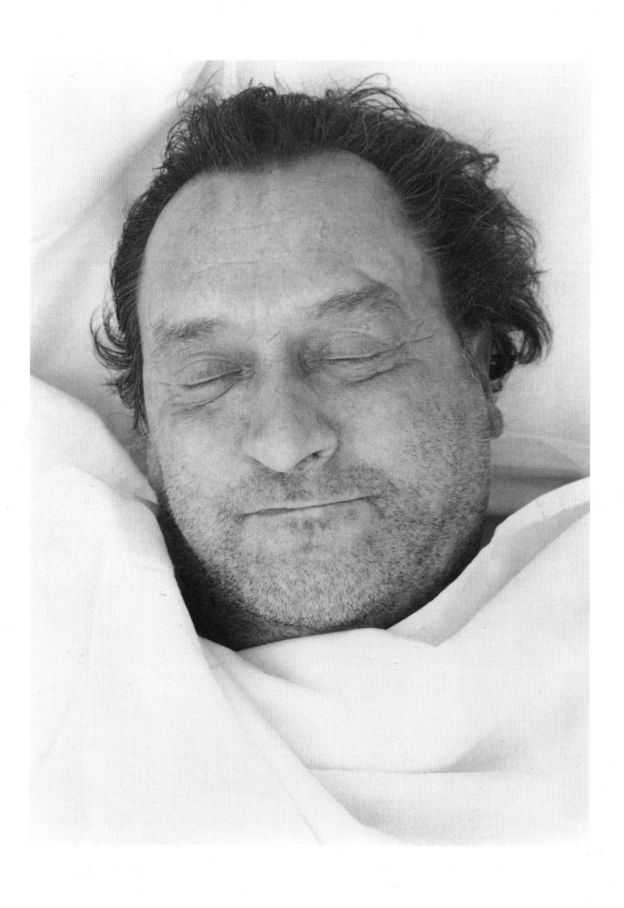

Facing Down

In *Facing Down* the photographer meets resistance from the subject, who refuses to co-operate or submit to the camera. Power struggles erupt as photographer and subject vie for control of the image. The subject confronts both the camera and the viewer, at times seeking our engagement, at other times defiant, even aggressive, trying to intimidate us, to face us down.

Previous page **Ingar Krauss.** *Untitled (Hannah), Ediger-Eller*, 2001 [56]
Below **Jorge Molder.** From the series *T.V.*, 1997 [83]
Right **Pierre Fantys.** *Mask II*, 1999 [27]

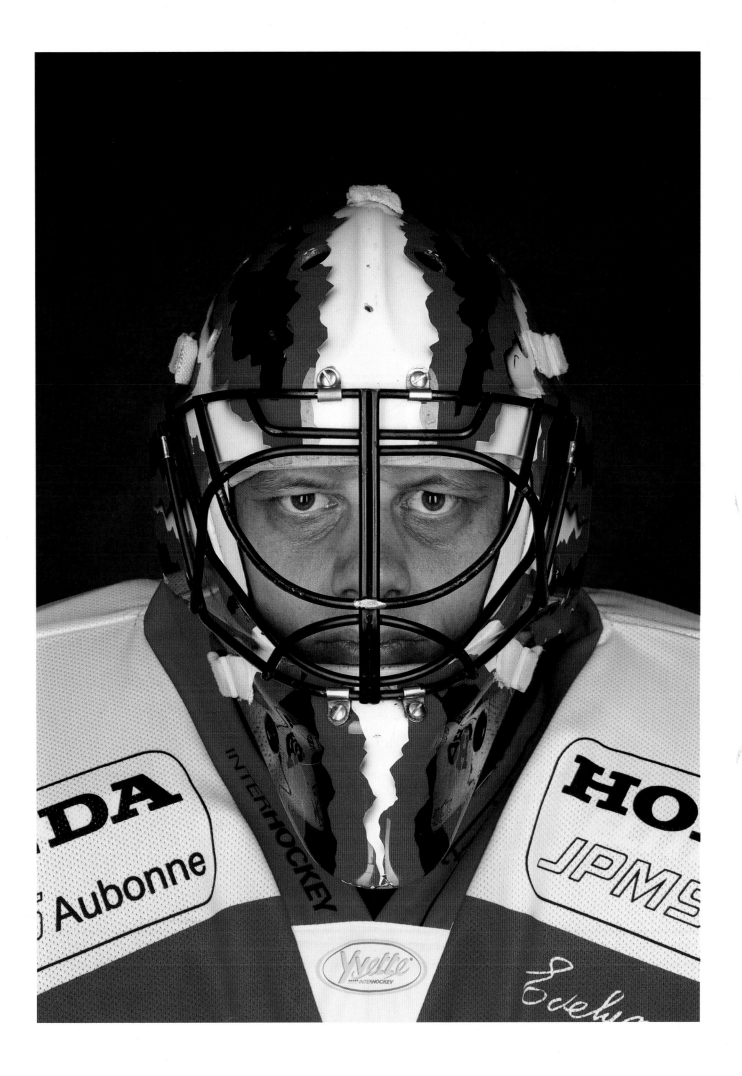

Exchanging Faces

Just as identity can be lost, it can also be assumed, swapped or re-invented. The artists and photographers in *Exchanging Faces* collude in this process, exploring, through composite, morphed or manipulated images – and other means of visual deceit – the possibilities of creating new personas, as false as they are believable. Fixed roles, gender, social and racial stereotypes are all called into question.

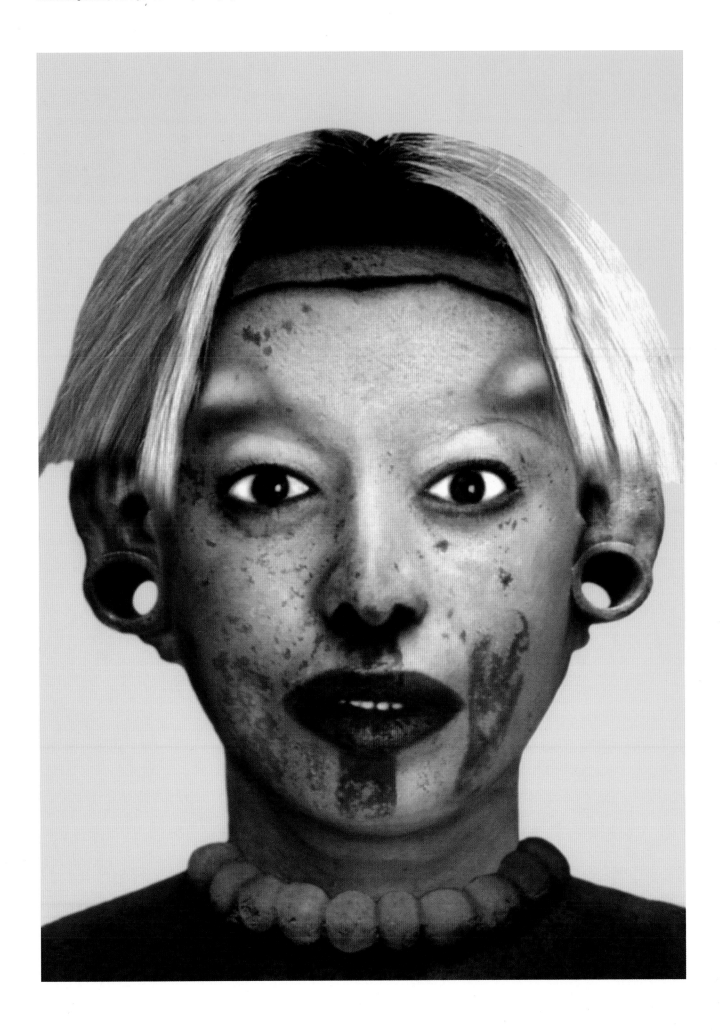

Human vanity is one of the most certain and profitable weaknesses of mankind … All those whose minds were empty and their pockets full … were pleased they could have their image multiplied. *Charles d'Audigier, c. 1870*

Valérie Belin. *Michael Jackson,* 2003 [11]

Below **Alison Jackson.** *Di, Dodi and Baby,* 1998 [44]
Right **Keith Cottingham.** *Fictitious Portraits,* 1992 [15]

Below **Tibor Kalman.** From the series *What if*. Published in *Colors* magazine (Issue 4), 1993 [46]
Right **Hee Jin Kang.** *Danny* from the series *Kissable*, 2001 [47]

what if..?
was wäre (wenn)..?

COLORS

Making Faces

The means to construct new faces and reconstruct existing ones – and the motives for doing so – are endless. Using a wide range of image-making procedures, from montage, composite images and multiple exposures to complex digital technologies, the truth and reality of appearance is questioned and overturned, and the powers of manipulation and artifice are openly celebrated.

Martin Parr. *Guadalahaja (Mexico)*, 2002-2003. From the series *Autoportrait*, 1999–2004 [93]

 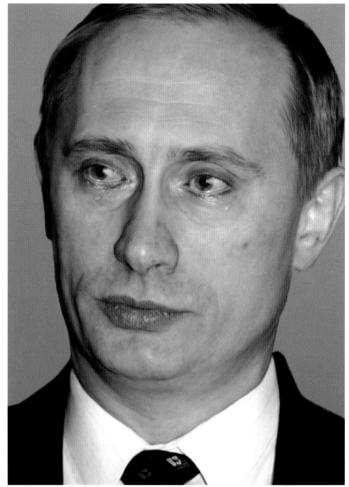

The human face is really like that of an oriental god, really a cluster of different faces, on different planes, which one never sees all at once.
Marcel Proust

Above **Helen Sear.** *2XJP* from the series *Twice…once*, 1998–2000 [115]
Right **Yotta Kippe.** *Precious Moments*, 2003 [52]

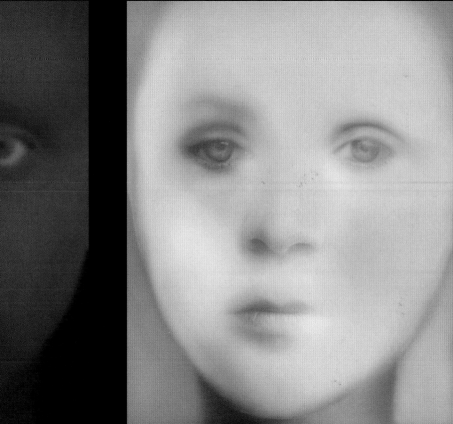

Faces On

Faces can be literally 'put on', and appearances constructed. Ideas and standards of beauty today are increasingly manipulable, and the beautician and cosmetic surgeon play a part alongside the photographer. In a world of increasing artificiality, life can be breathed into the mannequin and the corpse. Ultimately, ideals of beauty are revealed as having as much to do with the average, and common acceptance, as with the exceptional.

Thomas Dworzak. *Taliban portraits, Kandahar, Afghanistan* from the series *Taliban portraits*, 2002 [25]

Brooks Kraft. *Presidential Candidate George W. Bush, Television Interview, Los Angeles*, May 2000 [54]

There is, in the human face, an infinity of twists and turns and escape routes.
Georges Bataille

Raphael Hefti. *Esthéticiennes*, 2002 [37]

Previous page **Inez van Lamsweerde / Vinoodh Matadin.** *Björk (Poisson-Nageur)*, 2000 [64]
Below **Thomas Weisskopf.** From the series *Cut*, 2002 [122]

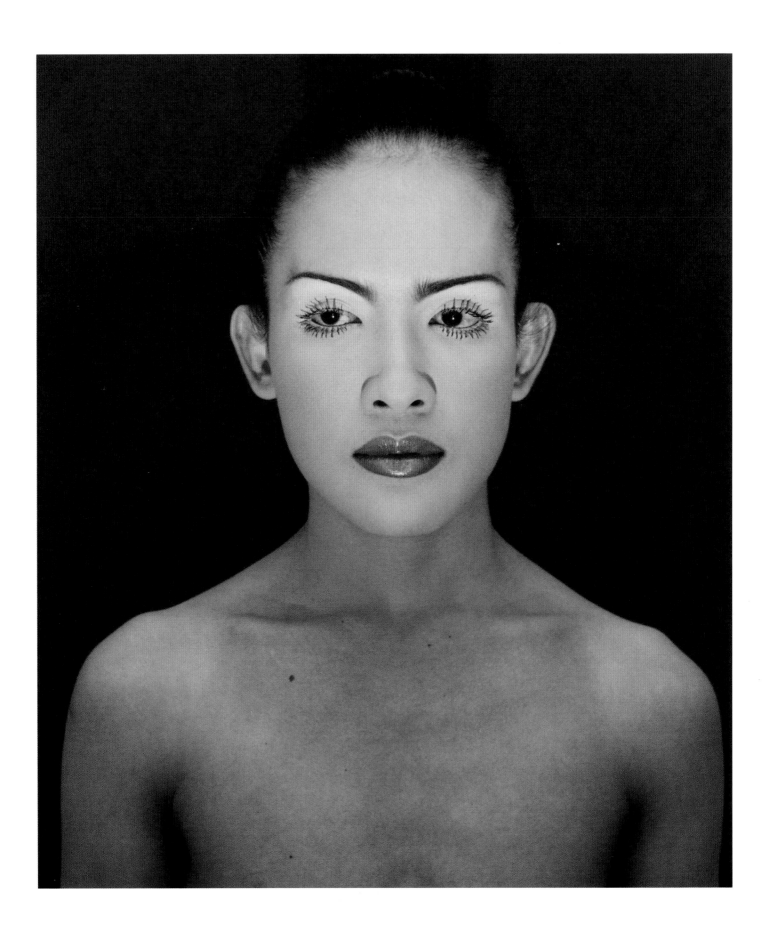

The theory of an ideal Beauty is tied to a period of history controlled by a religious or aristocratic power. In a democracy, the rules of aesthetics can be interpreted by each citizen.
Michel Melot
Beauty Industry Researcher

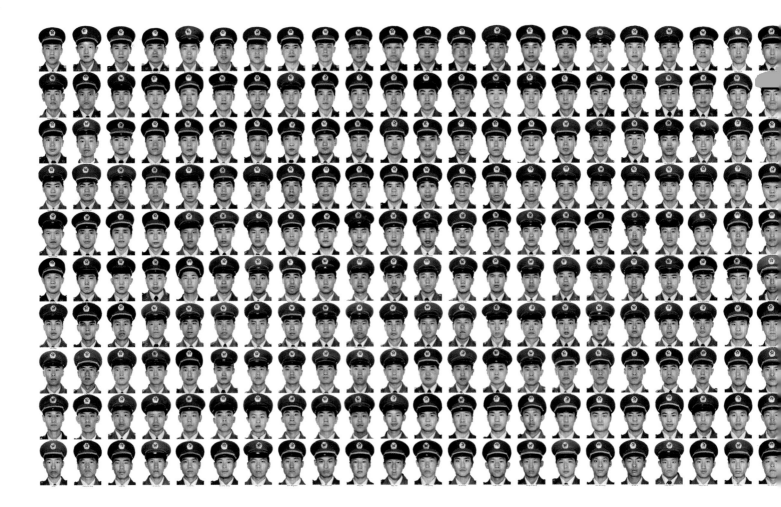

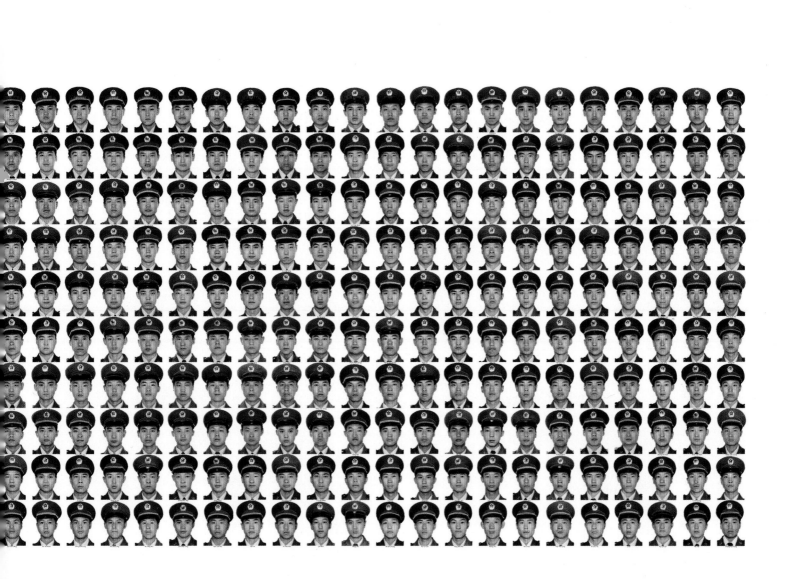

Charles Fréger. *Winner face* from the series *Steps*, 2001-02 [30]

The camera tends to turn people into things, and the photograph extends and multiplies the human image to the proportions of mass-produced merchandise. The movie stars and matinee idols are put into the public domain by photography. They become dreams that money can buy. They can be bought and thumbed more easily than public prostitutes. *Marshall McLuhan*

Valérie Belin. *Untitled*, 2001 [10]

Valérie Belin. *Untitled*, 2003 [12]

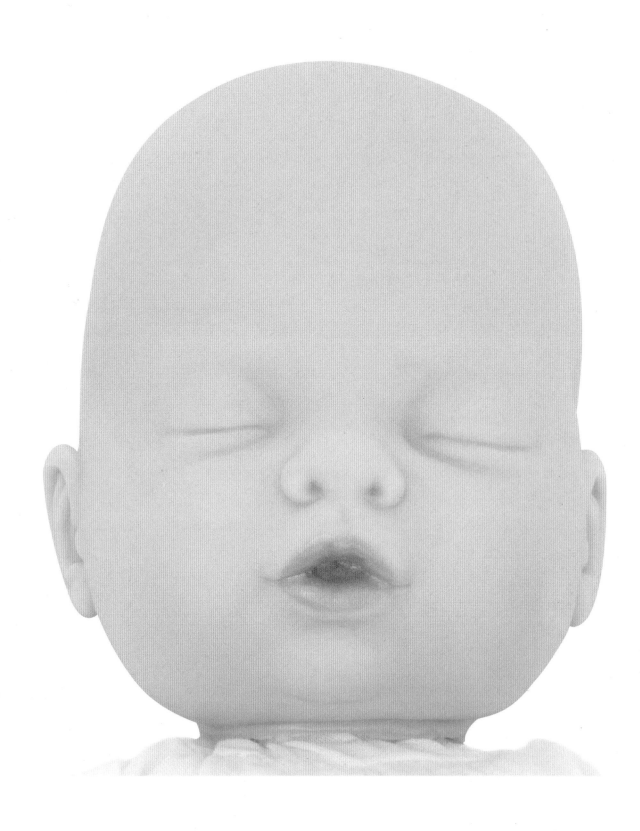

Above **Mona Schweizer.** *A Portrait of a Doll*, 2004 [113]
Right **Inez van Lamsweerde / Vinoodh Matadin.** *Kirsten*, 1997 [63]

Losing Face/Saving Face

Ideals of beauty, handed down by the media, fashion and advertising, are increasingly pervasive and persuasive, and attempts to conform to them can lead to the risk of anonymity, a loss of individuality, self-effacement. The artists and photographers in this section use a variety of strategies to explore this trend. Devices such as disguise, masking, retouching and the obliteration of distinguishing features are used to conceal or erase individual identities both literally and figuratively.

Loretta Lux. *Dorothea*, 2001 [74]

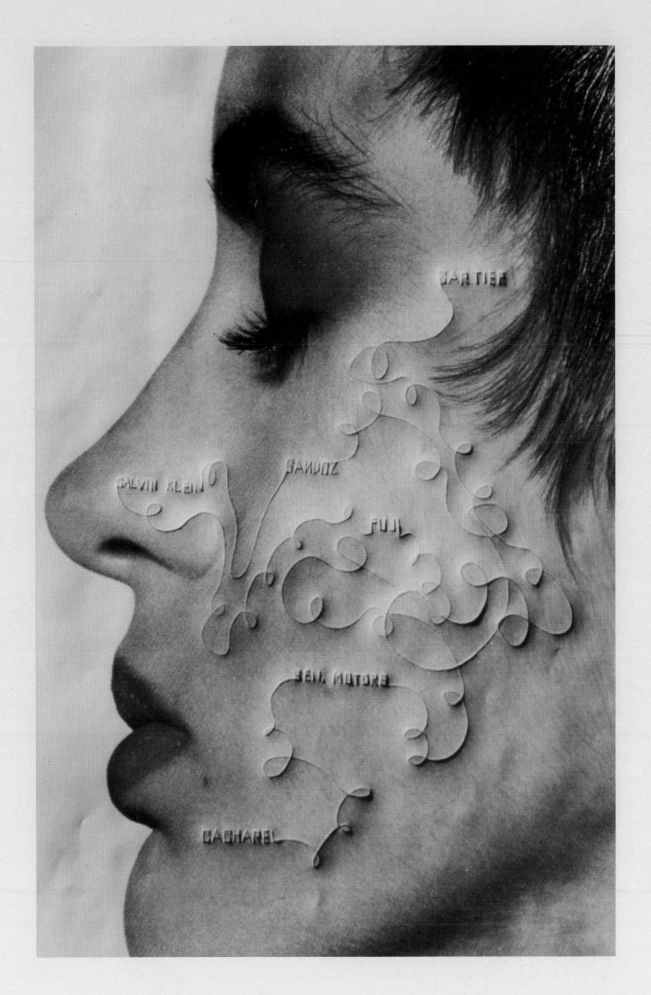

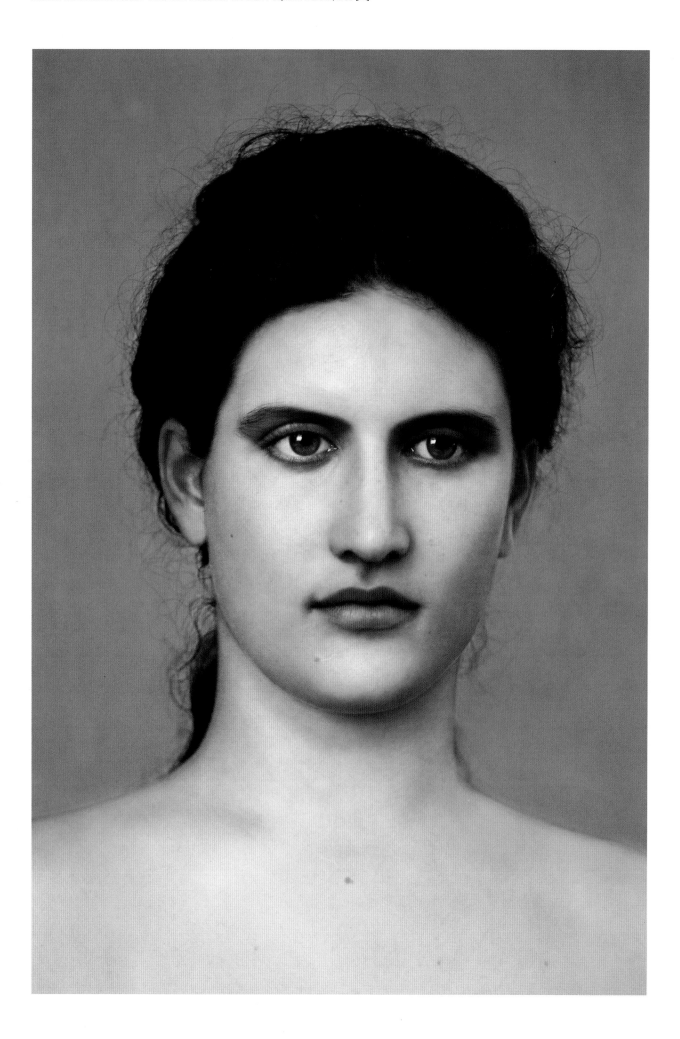

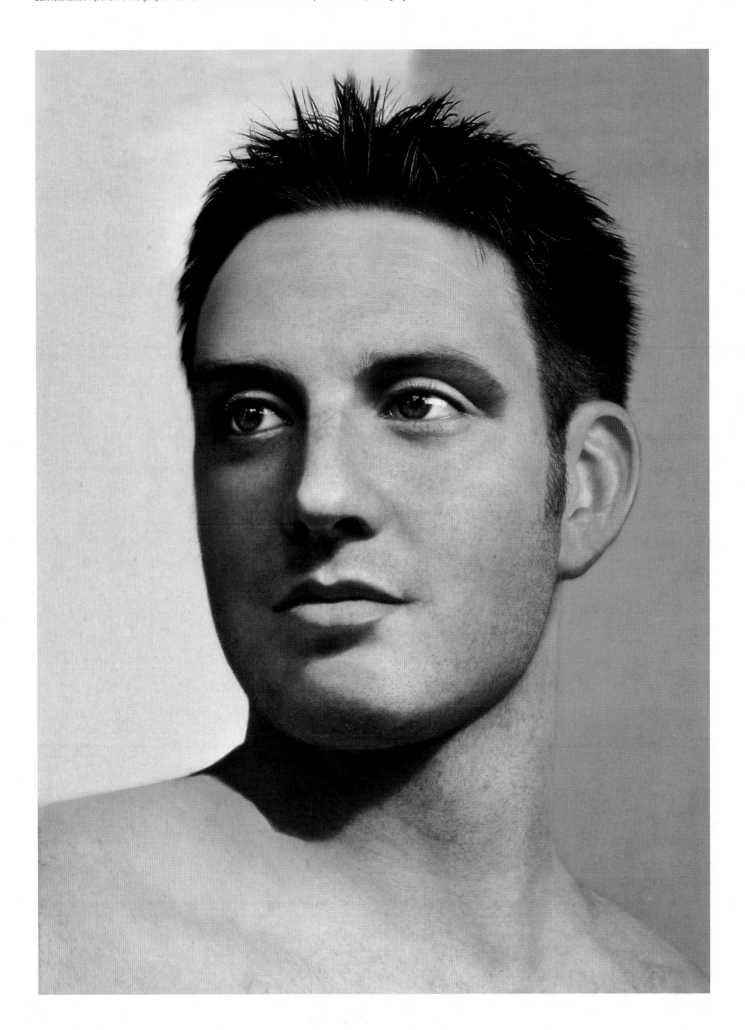

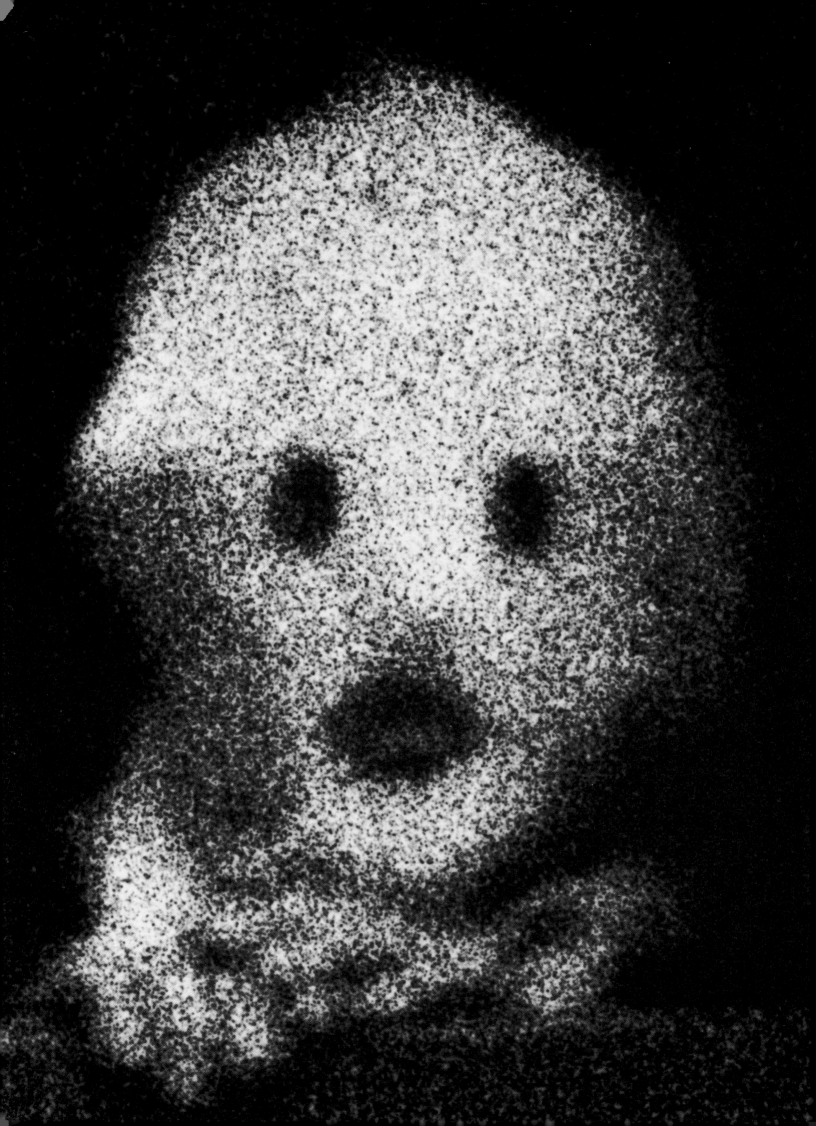

Whoever has followed the adventures of the image has, for ten, twenty, or thirty years witnessed the strange 'obliteration' of the human face.
Serge Daney
Historian and Film Critic

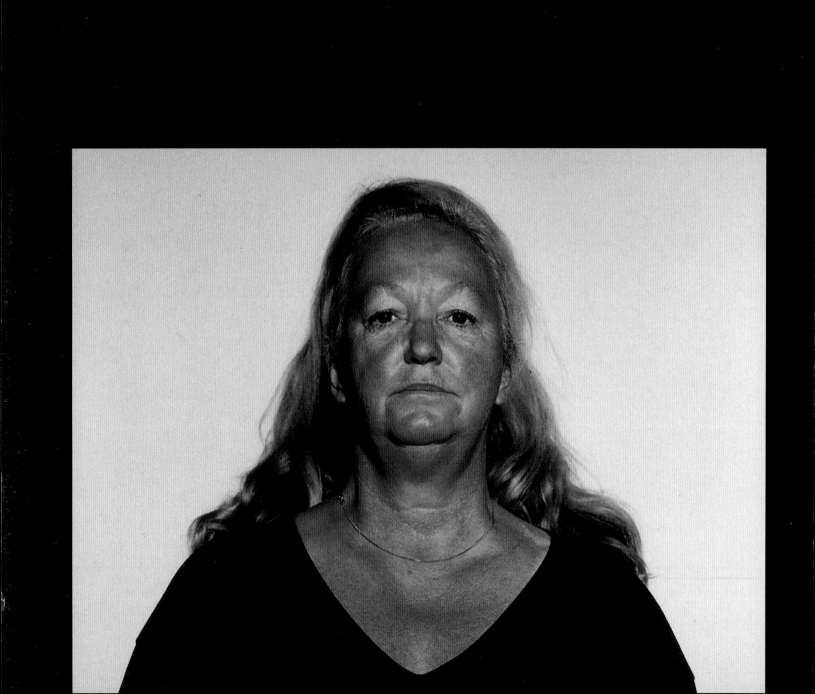

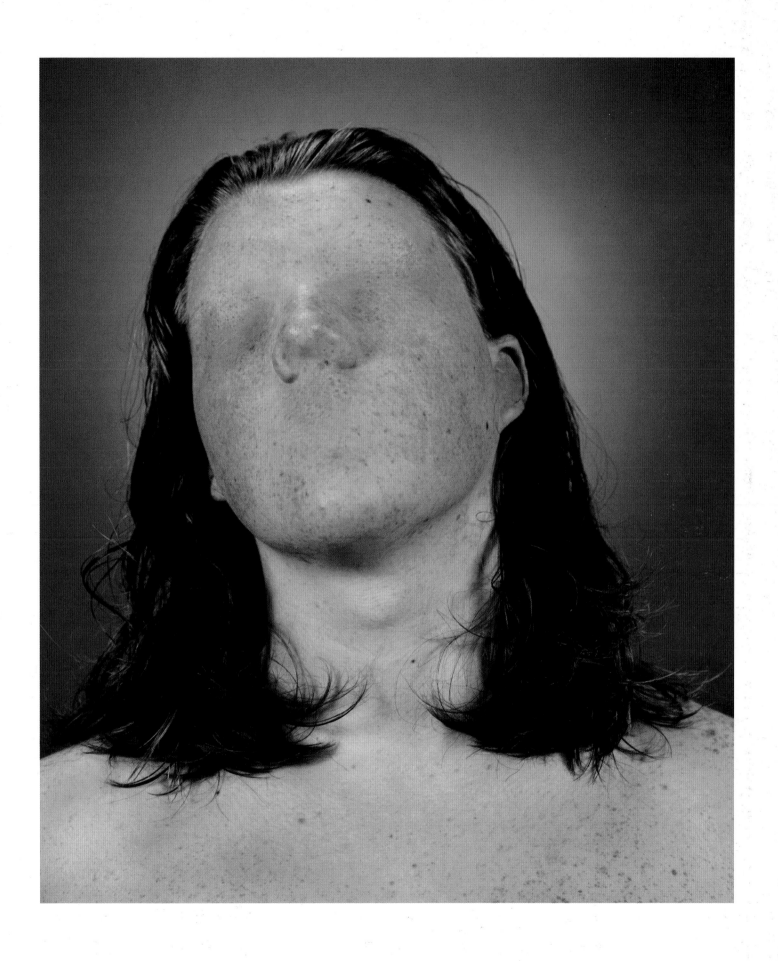

Left **Jean-Pierre Khazem.** *Pause 17*, 2002 [51]
Below **Gillian Wearing.** *Self-Portrait*, 2000 [121]

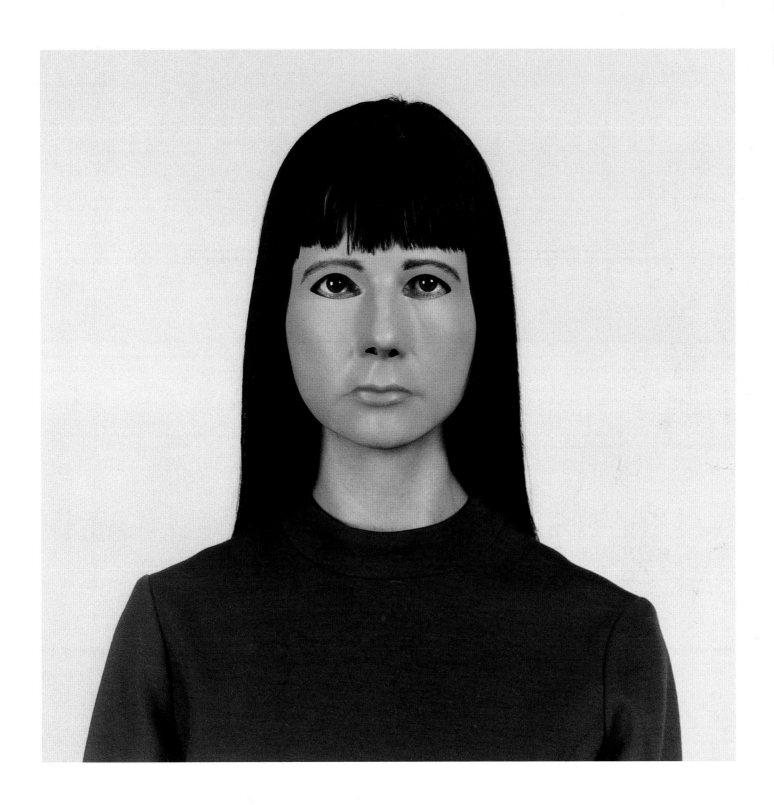

List of Works

All measurements are height x width x depth. Page references are to illustrations in this book.

In some instances more than one photograph in a series has been listed as one work. The actual number of works in the exhibition is 191.

1
Operation Iraqi Freedom Military Heroes Deck of Playing Cards, 2003
photomechanical prints;
dimensions variable
Courtesy of GreatUSAflags Patriot

2
The Iraqi 'Most Wanted' Deck of Playing Cards, 2003
photomechanical prints;
dimensions variable
Courtesy of GreatUSAflags Patriot

3
Yuri A (Brasil, b. 1961)
Life in Progress (Work in progress), 2003
digital print; 164 x 66 cm
Courtesy of the artist, Zurich

4
Yuri A (Brasil, b. 1961)
Life in Regress (Work in progress), 2003
digital print; 164 x 66 cm
Courtesy of the artist, Zurich

5 (p.51)
Bill Armstrong (USA, b. 1952)
Untitled, 2000–01
c-prints (6 photographs); each 61 x 45 cm
William Floyd Fine Art, New York
© Bill Armstrong 2004

6
Aziz + Cucher (Anthony Aziz, USA, b. 1961/
Sammy Cucher, Venezuela, b. 1958)
Maria from the series *DYSTOPIA,* 1994
digitised c-print; 93 x 73 cm
Galerie Yvonamor Palix, Paris

7 (p.81)
Aziz + Cucher (Anthony Aziz, USA, b. 1961/
Sammy Cucher, Venezuela, b. 1958)
Rick from the series *DYSTOPIA,* 1994
digitised c-print; 96 x 76 cm
Courtesy of Henry Urbach Gallery, New York and Galerie Yvonamor Palix, Paris
© Aziz + Cucher 1994/2004

8
Dorothée Baumann (Switzerland, b. 1972)
Face you, 2004
digital print; 74.5 x 92 cm
Courtesy of the artist, Switzerland

9
Philippe Bazin (France, b. 1954)
Nés, 1998
gelatin silver prints (6 photographs);
each 46 x 46 cm
Galerie Anne Barrault, Paris

10 (p.66)
Valérie Belin (France, b. 1964)
Untitled, 2001
gelatin silver prints (3 photographs);
each 100 x 80 cm
Galerie Xippas, Paris
© the artist 2001

11 (p.34)
Valérie Belin (France, b. 1964)
Michael Jackson, 2003
gelatin silver prints (4 photographs);
each 161 x 125 cm
Galerie Xippas, Paris
© the artist 2003

12 (p.67)
Valérie Belin (France, b. 1964)
Untitled, 2003
gelatin silver prints (3 photographs);
each 100 x 80 cm
Galerie Xippas, Paris
© the artist 2003

13 (p.73)
Daniele Buetti (Switzerland, b. 1956)
Looking for Love, 1996
manipulated photographs;
dimensions variable
Musée de l'Elysée, Lausanne

14 (p.33)
Nancy Burson (USA, b. 1948)
Warhead I, 1982
gelatin silver print (computer-generated composite); 18.5 x 19 cm
Musée de l'Elysée, Lausanne

15 (p.37)
Keith Cottingham (USA, b. 1965)
Fictitious Portraits, 1992
digital print; 155 x 134 cm
Courtesy Ronald Feldman Fine Arts, New York and Espace d'Art Yvonamor Palix, Paris
© Keith Cottingham 2004

16 (pp.42–43)
Jiří David (Czech Republic, b. 1956)
From the series *No compassion,* 2001
c-prints (10 photographs); each 80 x 57 cm
Musée de l'Elysée, Lausanne

17
Maya Dickerhof (Switzerland, b. 1970)
Untitled from the series *Memory,* 2001
c-print; 50 x 40 cm
Courtesy of the artist, Zurich

18
Philip-Lorca diCorcia (USA, b. 1953)
Heads #8, 2000
c-print; 125 x 155 cm
Galerie Rodolphe Janssen, Brussels

19
Philip-Lorca diCorcia (USA, b. 1953)
Heads #20, 2000
c-print; 125 x 155 cm
Galerie Rodolphe Janssen, Brussels

20
Philip-Lorca diCorcia (USA, b. 1953)
Heads #6, 2001
c-print; 125 x 155 cm
Galerie Rodolphe Janssen, Brussels

21 (p.20)
Rineke Dijkstra (The Netherlands, b. 1959)
Tia, Amsterdam, June 23, 1994
c-print; 62 x 52 cm
Marian Goodman Gallery, New York

22 (p.20)
Rineke Dijkstra (The Netherlands, b. 1959)
Tia, Amsterdam, November 14, 1994
c-print; 62 x 52 cm
Marian Goodman Gallery, New York

23 (p.28)
Désirée Dolron (The Netherlands, b. 1963)
Xteriors II, 2001
cibachrome print; 165 x 120 cm
Courtesy Michael Hoppen Gallery, London
© Désirée Dolron 2004

24 (p.46)
Chris Dorley-Brown (UK, b. 1958)
The Face of 2000, 2000
c-print (computer-generated composite);
76 x 101 cm
Courtesy of the artist, London
© Chris Dorley-Brown and Haverhill Town Council

25 (p.53)
Thomas Dworzak (Germany, b. 1972)
Taliban portraits, Kandahar, Afghanistan, from the series *Taliban portraits,* 2002
c-prints (3 photographs); 18 x 24 cm, 24 x 18 cm, 24 x 18 cm
Magnum Photos

26
Ger van Elk (The Netherlands, b. 1941)
Famous Hollywood Kissing, 2002
digital video, flatscreen; 56 x 62 cm
Galerie Durand-Dessert, Paris

27 (p.27)
Pierre Fantys (Switzerland, b. 1961)
Mask II, 1999
lamda print; 170 x 120 cm
Courtesy of the artist, Switzerland

28 (pp.62–63)
Roland Fischer (Germany, b. 1958)
Soldiers from the series
Group portraits, 2002
c-print; 125 x 410 cm
Galerie Sollertis, Toulouse

29
Frank Fournier (France, b. 1948)
Cape Canaveral. During the explosion of space shuttle Challenger, the wife of the captain with President Ronald Reagan and his wife, 1986
c-print; 40 x 60 cm
Musée de l'Elysée, Lausanne

30 (p.64)
Charles Fréger (France, b. 1975)
Winner face from the series *Steps,* 2001–02
c-prints (7 photographs); each 59 x 49 cm
Galerie 779, Paris

31 (p.17)
Lee Friedlander (USA, b. 1934)
Finland, 1995
gelatin silver print; 40 x 50 cm
Galerie Thomas Zander, Köln/Fraenkel Gallery, San Francisco

32
Lee Friedlander (USA, b. 1934)
Ayers Cliff, Canada, 1997
gelatin silver print; 40 x 50 cm
Galerie Thomas Zander, Köln/Fraenkel Gallery, San Francisco

33
Lee Friedlander (USA, b. 1934)
Davis Mountains, Texas, 1997
gelatin silver print; 40 x 50 cm
Galerie Thomas Zander, Köln/Fraenkel Gallery, San Francisco

34
Paul Graham (UK, b. 1956)
Red Eyes, 1999
c-prints (10 photographs); each 25 x 35 cm
Galerie Bob van Orsouw, Zurich

35 (p.72)
Kathy Grove (USA, b. 1948)
The Other Series: After Lange, 1989–90
gelatin silver print; 49 x 38.5 cm
Musée de l'Elysée, Lausanne

36
Ron Haviv (USA, b. 1948)
A defaced photograph found by a Bosnian family when they returned to their home in a Sarajevo suburb, Spring 1996
c-print; 40 x 30 cm
Ron Haviv/VII

37 (pp.56–57)
Raphael Hefti (Switzerland, b. 1976)
Esthéticiennes, 2002
ilfochrome prints (7 photographs);
each 90 x 75 cm
Courtesy of the artist, Zurich
© Raphael Hefti/écal 2002

38
Elizabeth Heyert (USA, b. 1951)
Daphne Jones (Born August 1954, Harlem NY, Died January 2004, Harlem NY) from the series *Going to the Party,* 2004
c-print; 101.6 x 76.2 cm
Edwynn Houk Gallery, New York

39
Elizabeth Heyert (USA, b. 1951)
James 'La Smoothe' Patterson Jr. (Born September 1966, Harlem NY, Died February 2004, Harlem NY) from the series *Going to the Party,* 2004
c-print; 101. 6 x 76.2 cm
Edwynn Houk Gallery, New York

40
Elizabeth Heyert (USA, b. 1951)
Raymond E. Jones Sr. (Born December 1928, Memphis TN, Died January 2004, Harlem NY) from the series *Going to the Party,* 2004
c-print; 101.6 x 76.2 cm
Edwynn Houk Gallery, New York

41
John Hilliard (UK, b. 1945)
Blonde, 1996
cibachrome print; 130 x 176 cm
Courtesy of the artist, London

42
Ralph T. Hutchings (UK, b. 1945)
Internal view showing arterial blood supply of a baby's head, n.d.
lightbox; dimensions variable
Courtesy of the artist, London

43
Ralph T. Hutchings (UK, b. 1945)
Coronal section of the head, 1996
lightbox; dimensions variable
Courtesy of the artist, London

44 (p.36)
Alison Jackson (UK)
Di, Dodi and Baby, 1998
gelatin silver print; 122 x 122 cm
Program, London

45
Alison Jackson (UK)
Charles, Camilla and Diana, 1999
gelatin silver prints (5 photographs);
each 50.8 x 76.2 cm
Program, London

46 (p.38)
Tibor Kalman (USA, b. in Hungary, 1949–99)
From the series *What if*. Published in *Colors* magazine (Issue 4), 1993
magazine tear sheets; each 30.5 x 28 cm
Musée de l'Elysée, Lausanne

47 (p.39)
Hee Jin Kang (Korea, b. 1974)
Danny from the series *Kissable*, 2001
c-print; 76 x 76 cm
Courtesy Michael Hoppen Gallery, London
© Hee Jin Kang 2004

48
Hee Jin Kang (Korea, b. 1974)
Francis from the series *Kissable*, 2001
c-print; 76 x 76 cm
Courtesy Michael Hoppen Gallery, London

49
Hee Jin Kang (Korea, b. 1974)
Vishal from the series *Kissable*, 2001
c-print; 76 x 76 cm
Courtesy Michael Hoppen Gallery, London

50
Jean-Pierre Khazem (France, b. 1968)
Pause 13, 2002
c-print; 125 x 154 cm
Farfabriken, Stockholm/Galerie Emmanuel Perrotin, Paris

51 (p.82)
Jean-Pierre Khazem (France, b. 1968)
Pause 17, 2002
c-print; 125 x 154 cm
Farfabriken, Stockholm/Galerie Emmanuel Perrotin, Paris
© Jean-Pierre Khazem 2004

52 (p.49)
Yotta Kippe (Germany, b. 1971)
Precious Moments, 2003
digital prints on audibond (6 photographs); each 90 x 70 cm
Galerie Blickensdorff, Berlin

53
Micha Klein (The Netherlands, b. 1964)
Classic Artificial Beauty (The original sequence), 1998–2003
DVD
Torch Gallery, Amsterdam

54 (p.54)
Brooks Kraft (USA)
Presidential Candidate George W. Bush, Television Interview, Los Angeles, May 2000
c-print; 75 x 114 cm
Courtesy of the artist, USA

55
Ingar Krauss (Germany, b. 1965)
Untitled (Hannah), Zechin, 2000
gelatin silver print; 75 x 61 cm
Courtesy of the artist, Berlin

56 (p.25)
Ingar Krauss (Germany, b. 1965)
Untitled (Hannah), Ediger-Eller, 2001
gelatin silver print; 75 x 61 cm
Courtesy of the artist, Berlin

57
Ingar Krauss (Germany, b. 1965)
Untitled (Hannah), Zechin, 2001
gelatin silver print; 75 x 61 cm
Courtesy of the artist, Berlin

58
Ingar Krauss (Germany, b. 1965)
Untitled (Nico), Zechin, 2001
gelatin silver print; 75 x 61 cm
Courtesy of the artist, Berlin

59
Ingar Krauss (Germany, b. 1965)
Untitled (Luca), Zechin, 2002
gelatin silver print; 75 x 61 cm
Courtesy of the artist, Berlin

60 (p.29)
Marie-Jo Lafontaine (Belgium, b. 1950)
Savoir, retenir et fixer ce qui est sublime #09, 1989
gelatin silver print, oil on wood;
200 x 120 cm
Galerie Mai 36, Zurich

61
Marie-Jo Lafontaine (Belgium, b. 1950)
Savoir, retenir et fixer ce qui est sublime #10, 1989
gelatin silver print, oil on wood;
200 x 120 cm
Galerie Mai 36, Zurich

62
Marie-Jo Lafontaine (Belgium, b. 1950)
Savoir, retenir et fixer ce qui est sublime #14, 1989
gelatin silver print, oil on wood;
200 x 120 cm
Galerie Mai 36, Zurich

63 (p.69)
Inez van Lamsweerde/Vinoodh Matadin (The Netherlands, van Lamsweerde b. 1963 /Matadin b. 1961)
Kirsten, 1997
c-print; 50 x 50 cm
Courtesy of the artists and Matthew Marks Gallery, New York

64 (pp.58-59)
Inez van Lamsweerde/Vinoodh Matadin (The Netherlands, van Lamsweerde b. 1963/Matadin b. 1961)
Björk (Poisson-Nageur), 2000
c-print; 127 x 157 cm
Courtesy of the artists and Matthew Marks Gallery, New York

65 (p.47)
Eva Lauterlein (Switzerland, b. 1977)
chimères, 2002
lamda c-prints (3 photographs);
each 75 x 75 cm
Musée de l'Elysée, Lausanne

66
LawickMüller (Germany, Friederike van Lawick b. 1958/Hans Müller b. 1954)
Portrait of artist duos: Muriel Olesen/ Gérald Minkoff from the series *La Folie à Deux*, 1996
digitally-processed photographs (16 photographs); 27.5 x 20.5 cm
Musée de l'Elysée, Lausanne

67
LawickMüller (Germany, Friederike van Lawick b. 1958/Hans Müller b. 1954)
Apollo from Olympia – Florian from the series *PERFECTLY superNATURAL*, 1999
cibachrome print; 80 x 59 cm
Galerie Patricia Dorfmann, Paris

68
LawickMüller (Germany, Friederike van Lawick b. 1958/Hans Müller b. 1954)
Apollo from Olympia – Micha from the series *PERFECTLY superNATURAL*, 1999
cibachrome print; 80 x 59 cm
Galerie Patricia Dorfmann, Paris

69 (p.75)
LawickMüller (Germany, Friederike van Lawick b. 1958/Hans Müller b. 1954)
Apollo from Olympia – Oliver from the series *PERFECTLY superNATURAL*, 1999
cibachrome print; 80 x 59 cm
Galerie Patricia Dorfmann, Paris

70
LawickMüller (Germany, Friederike van Lawick b. 1958/Hans Müller b. 1954)
Athena Velletri – Anna from the series *PERFECTLY superNATURAL*, 1999
cibachrome print; 100 x 67 cm
Galerie Patricia Dorfmann, Paris

71 (p.74)
LawickMüller (Germany, Friederike van Lawick b. 1958/Hans Müller b. 1954)
Athena Velletri – Nina from the series *PERFECTLY superNATURAL*, 1999
cibachrome print; 100 x 67 cm
Galerie Patricia Dorfmann, Paris

72
LawickMüller (Germany, Friederike van Lawick b. 1958/Hans Müller b. 1954)
Athena Velletri – Simone from the series *PERFECTLY superNATURAL*, 1999
cibachrome print; 100 x 67 cm
Galerie Patricia Dorfmann, Paris

73
Sarah Leen (USA)
The Mask, 2002
inkjet print; 33 x 48 cm
Courtesy of the artist, USA

74 (p.71)
Loretta Lux (Germany, b. 1969)
Dorothea, 2001
ilfochrome print; 50 x 50 cm
Courtesy Yossi Milo Gallery, New York

75
Loretta Lux (Germany, b. 1969)
Isabella, 2001
ilfochrome print; 50 x 50 cm
Courtesy Yossi Milo Gallery, New York

76
Sally Mann (USA, b. 1951)
Jessie as Jessie, 1990
gelatin silver print; 50 x 61 cm
Edwynn Houk Gallery, New York

77
Sally Mann (USA, b. 1951)
Jessie as Madonna, 1990
gelatin silver print; 50 x 61 cm
Edwynn Houk Gallery, New York

78 (p.78)
Claudia Matzko (USA, b. 1958)
Voices #2, 2002
cibachrome print; 31 x 25 cm
Courtesy of the artist and Angles Gallery, Santa Monica, CA

79
Claudia Matzko (USA, b. 1958)
Voices #3, 2002
cibachrome print; 31 x 25 cm
Courtesy of the artist and Angles Gallery, Santa Monica, CA

80
Claudia Matzko (USA, b. 1958)
Voices #5, 2002
cibachrome print; 31 x 25 cm
Courtesy of the artist and Angles Gallery, Santa Monica, CA

81
Jorge Molder (Portugal, b. 1947)
From the series *T.V.*, 1995–96
gelatin silver print; 102 x 102 cm
Collection of Banco Privado Português

82
Jorge Molder (Portugal, b. 1947)
From the series *T.V.*, 1995–96
gelatin silver print; 102 x 102 cm
Collection of Banco Privado Português

83 (p.26)
Jorge Molder (Portugal, b. 1947)
From the series *T.V.*, 1997
gelatin silver print; 102 x 102 cm
Private Collection, Portugal

84
Jorge Molder (Portugal, b. 1947)
Untitled from the series *Attenuating Circumstances*, 2003
gelatin silver print; 122 x 122 cm
Lisboa 20 arte contemporânea, Lisbon

85
Vik Muniz (Brazil, b. 1961)
Grey Marilyn from the series *Pictures of Diamond Dust*, 2003
cibachrome print; 101 x 93 cm
Galerie Xippas, Paris

86
Vik Muniz (Brazil, b. 1961)
Reversal Grey Marilyn from the series *Pictures of Diamond Dust*, 2003
cibachrome print; 101 x 93 cm
Galerie Xippas, Paris

87 (p.76)
José Luís Neto (Portugal, b. 1966)
From the series *22474*, 2000
gelatin silver prints (24 photographs);
each 41 x 31 cm
Módulo – Centro Difusor de Arte, Lisboa e Porto. Arquivo Fotográfico Municipal de Lisboa

88 (p.77)
José Luís Neto (Portugal, b. 1966)
From the series *22475*, 2003
gelatin silver prints (24 photographs);
each 41 x 31 cm
Módulo – Centro Difusor de Arte, Lisboa e Porto. Arquivo Fotográfico Municipal de Lisboa

89 (p.23)
Adriënne M. Norman (USA, b. 1964)
Naomi Oron from the series *Skin Portraits*, 2001–03
c-print; 100 x 100 cm
Courtesy of the artist, Amsterdam

90 (p.80)
Anneè Olofsson (Sweden, b. 1966)
I put my foot deep in the tracks that you made, 2000
c-print; 105 x 140 cm
Mia Sundberg Gallery, Stockholm

91
Orlan (France, b. 1947)
Refiguration/Self-Hybridation #22, 1999
cibachrome print; 150 x 100 cm
Courtesy of the artist, Paris

92 (p.31)
Orlan (France, b. 1947)
Refiguration/Self-Hybridation #30, 1999
cibachrome print; 150 x 100 cm
Courtesy of the artist, Paris

93 (p.41)
Martin Parr (UK, b. 1952)
From the series *Autoportrait*, 1999–2004
c-prints and gelatin silver prints (21 photographs); dimensions variable
Magnum Photos

94
Emmanuelle Purdon (France, b. 1965)
Hearts are trumps (from a painting by Sir John Everett Millais, Tate Gallery) from the series *Femmes de mystère*, 1997
gelatin silver print; 30.5 x 24 cm
Musée de l'Elysée, Lausanne

95
Emmanuelle Purdon (France, b. 1965)
La comtesse Rimsky Korsakoff (from a painting by F. Xavier Winterhalter) from the series *Femmes de mystère*, 1997
gelatin silver print; 30.5 x 24 cm
Musée de l'Elysée, Lausanne

96
Emmanuelle Purdon (France, b. 1965)
La Liégeoise (from an anonymous painter) from the series *Femmes de mystère*, 1997
gelatin silver print; 30.5 x 24 cm
Musée de l'Elysée, Lausanne

97
Emmanuelle Purdon (France, b. 1965)
Mme Kuffearth (from a painting by Gouwelooss, Musée Charlier, Bruxelles) from the series *Femmes de mystère*, 1997
gelatin silver print; 30.5 x 24 cm
Musée de l'Elysée, Lausanne

98
Emmanuelle Purdon (France, b. 1965)
Ophélie (from a painting by Ernest Hébert, Musée Hébert, Paris) from the series *Femmes de mystère*, 1997
gelatin silver print; 30.5 x 24 cm
Musée de l'Elysée, Lausanne

99
Emmanuelle Purdon (France, b. 1965)
Sérénité (from a painting by Brusserat, Musée des Beaux-Arts de Tournai) from the series *Femmes de mystère*, 1997
gelatin silver print; 30.5 x 24 cm
Musée de l'Elysée, Lausanne

100 (p.32)
Pierre Radisic (Belgium, b. 1958)
Couple 8-5-82, 1982
gelatin silver prints (2 photographs, 1 postcard); photographs each 19 x 15.5 cm, postcard 15 x 11 cm
Courtesy of the artist, Brussels
© Pierre Radisic 1982

101 (p.19)
Judith Joy Ross (USA, b. 1946)
P.F.C. Maria I. Leon, U.S. Army Reserve, On Red Alert, Gulf War, 1990
gold-toned gelatin silver print; 24 x 19 cm
Pace/MacGill Gallery, New York

102
Karen Rowantree (Canada, b. Smiley 1947)
Bradley J. Sanborn from the series *Cheque Cashing Identification Photographs, Star Market Co., Boston*, 1976
gelatin silver prints (2 photographs);
each 51 x 41 cm
Collection of the artist, Canada

103
Karen Rowantree (Canada, b. Smiley 1947)
Martha Ann Wallen from the series *Cheque Cashing Identification Photographs, Star Market Co., Boston*, 1976
gelatin silver prints (2 photographs);
each 51 x 41 cm
Collection of the artist, Canada

104
Karen Rowantree (Canada, b. Smiley 1947)
Sandra M. Bushingham from the series *Cheque Cashing Identification Photographs, Star Market Co., Boston*, 1976
gelatin silver prints (2 photographs);
each 51 x 41 cm
Collection of the artist, Canada

105
Karen Rowantree (Canada, b. Smiley 1947)
Sonia Goldman from the series *Cheque Cashing Identification Photographs, Star Market Co., Boston*, 1976
gelatin silver prints (2 photographs);
each 51 x 41 cm
Collection of the artist, Canada

106
Karen Rowantree (Canada, b. Smiley 1947)
Susan K. Luciani from the series *Cheque Cashing Identification Photographs, Star Market Co., Boston*, 1976
gelatin silver prints (2 photographs);
each 51 x 41 cm
Collection of the artist, Canada

107
Thomas Ruff (Germany, b. 1958)
Other Portrait #143/146, 1994–95
silkscreen on paper; 205 x 155 cm
Galerie Mai 36, Zurich

108 (p.18)
Thomas Ruff (Germany, b. 1958)
Portrait (A. Koschkarow), 1999
c-print; 210 x 165 cm
Galerie Mai 36, Zurich
© DACS 2004

109
Sam Samore (USA, b. 1963)
Tower, 1999
gelatin silver prints (5 photographs);
each 75 x 115 cm
NSM Vie/ABN AMRO Collection

110
Tomoko Sawada (Japan, b. 1977)
ID 400, 1998
gelatin silver prints (100 photographs);
each 11.4 x 8.9 cm
The Third Gallery Aya, Osaka Japan

111 (p.22)
Rudolf Schaefer (Germany, b. 1952)
From the series *Dead Faces*, 1986
platinum prints (4 photographs);
each 22.5 x 16.5 cm
Musée de l'Elysée, Lausanne
© Rudolf Schaefer 1986

112 (p.44)
Gary Schneider (South Africa, b. 1954)
Helen, 2000
c-print; 153 x 122 cm
Julie Saul Gallery, New York

113 (p.68)
Mona Schweizer (Switzerland, b. 1978)
A Portrait of a Doll, 2004
lamda print; 70 x 70 cm
Courtesy of the artist, Switzerland

114
Helen Sear (UK, b. 1955)
2XLP from the series *Twice...once*, 1998–2000
gelatin silver print; 102 x 94 cm
Courtesy of the artist, London

115 (p.48)
Helen Sear (UK, b. 1955)
2XJP from the series *Twice...once*, 1998–2000
gelatin silver print; 102 x 94 cm
Courtesy of the artist, London

116
Darren Staples (UK)
Iranian asylum-seeker Abas Amini sits with his eyes, mouth and ears sewn up at his home in Nottingham, 27 May 2003
digital print; 28 x 37.5 cm
Reuters/Darren Staples

117 (p.50)
John Stezaker (UK, b. 1949)
Angel 2, 1997–99
iris print; 118 x 157 cm
Courtesy of the artist, London

118
John Stezaker (UK, b. 1949)
Angel 4, 1997–99
iris print; 118 x 157 cm
Courtesy of the artist, London

119
John Stezaker (UK, b. 1949)
Demon, 1997–99
iris print; 118 x 157 cm
Courtesy of the artist, London

120
Robert Walker (Canada)
Times Square, New York, 2002
c-print; 63 x 97 cm
Courtesy of the artist, Montreal

121 (p.83)
Gillian Wearing (UK, b. 1963)
Self-Portrait, 2000
c-print; 172 x 172 cm
Courtesy Maureen Paley Interim Art, London

122 (p.60)
Thomas Weisskopf (Switzerland, b. 1969)
From the series *Cut*, 2002
c-prints (6 photographs); each 50 x 43 cm
Galerie Römerapotheke, Zurich
© Thomas Weisskopf 2004

123
Patrick Witty (USA)
New Yorkers, September 11, 2001
gelatin silver print; 29 x 43 cm
Musée de l'Elysée, Lausanne

List of Lenders

VII Photo Agency, Paris
Américo Marques dos Santos, Cascais
Angles Gallery, Santa Monica
Ars Futura Galerie, Zurich
Artsadmin, London
Banco Privado Português, Lisbon
The Box Associati, Torino
Centro Português de Fotografia, Porto
DDH Foundation, Amsterdam
Edson Williams, Amsterdam
Edwynn Houk Gallery, New York
Espace d'art Yvonamor Palix, Paris
Fondation NSM Vie/ABN AMRO, Paris
Fraenkel Gallery, San Francisco
Francesco Solari, Paris
Galeria Berini, Barcelona
Galeria Pedro Oliveira, Porto
Galerie 213 Marion de Beaupré, Paris
Galerie 779, Paris
Galerie Anne Barrault, Paris
Galerie Anne de Villepoix, Paris
Galerie Blickensdorff, Berlin
Galerie Bob van Orsouw, Zurich
Galerie Bodo Niemann, Berlin
Galerie Domi Nostrae, Lyon
Galerie Donzé Van Saanen,
    Lausanne
Galerie Emmanuel Perrotin, Paris
Galerie Esther Woerdehoff, Paris
Galerie Jérôme de Noirmont, Paris
Galerie Liliane &
    Michel Durand-Dessert, Paris
Galerie Mai 36, Zurich
Galerie Minerva, Zurich
Galerie Patricia Dorfmann, Paris
Galerie Rodolphe Janssen, Brussels
Galerie Römerapotheke, Zurich

Galerie Sollertis, Toulouse
Galerie Thaddaeus Ropac, Paris
Galerie Thomas Zander, Cologne
Galerie Xippas, Paris
Galleria Il Torchio, Milan
gb agency, Paris
Institute of Contemporary Art, Portland
Josée et Marc Gensollen, Marseille
Julie Saul Gallery, New York
Katia et Emilio Bordoli, Como
Lisboa 20 arte contemporânea, Lisbon
L'Oeil Public, Paris
Lookat Photos, Zurich
Magnum Photos, Paris/London
Marian Goodman Gallery, New York
Matthew Marks Gallery, New York
Maureen Paley Interim Art, London
Mia Sundberg Gallery, Stockholm
Michael Hoppen Gallery, London
migros museum for
    Contemporary Art, Zurich
Musée de l'Elysée, Lausanne
Museu Serralves, Porto
Noirmont Prospect, Paris
Pace/MacGill Gallery, New York
Program, London
Reuters, Zurich /London
Richard Salmon Gallery, London
Roy Greenspan, Zurich
Scalo Books & Looks, Zurich/New York
Susan Hobbs Gallery, Toronto
The Third Gallery Aya, Osaka
Torch Gallery, Amsterdam
VG Bild-Kunst, Bonn
William Floyd Fine Art, New York
Yossi Milo Gallery, New York
Zabriskie Gallery, New York

With thanks to all of the artists and
photographers who have lent their works
to this exhibition.